Sentences can be very long, very short or somewhere in between.

This sentence is only two words.

Mog knits.

This word tells you who the sentence is about. The person or thing that the sentence is about is called the **subject** of the sentence.

This word tells you what the person is doing. Words that tell you what someone or something is doing are called **verbs.**

Nearly all sentences have at least a subject and a verb.

The sentence above does not tell you very much. The sentence below gives you a bit more information.

Mog knits hats.

This word tells you what is being knitted. The person or thing that the verb is happening to is called the **object** of the sentence.

Zog Og is trying to decide which of these words are verbs. Can you help him by putting a ring around the verbs?

car

street

climb

laugh

horse

throw

dance

jump

Meet the Ogs

Grandma Og

Grandma Og is very musical. She started playing the stonepipe when she was a girl.

Grandpa Og

Grandpa Og enjoys driving his rockmobile around the countryside.

Mrs. Og

Mrs. Og is a coin collector. She has over two hundred coins in her collection.

Mr. Og

Mr. Og likes cooking. His speciality is swampburger with tomato and pickle.

Mog Og

Mog Og enjoys writing. Her poems are often used in the school magazine.

Zog Og

Zog Og is very adventurous. Every week he has a mammoth riding lesson.

Can you use these words to make up a sentence about each of the Ogs?

writes

a rockmobile

a stonepipe

Mrs. Og

poems

coins

Mr. Og

drives

Zog Og

mammoths

eats

Grandma Og

Mog Og

Grandpa Og

plays

swampburgers

collects

rides

Write your sentences here.

Can you draw a straight line under the subject of each sentence?

Draw a ring around each verb.

Draw a wiggly line under the object in each sentence.

5

Nouns

Zog is daydreaming during a lesson at school. The teacher, Miss Spell, has written some words on the board. She asks Zog to put a star by the ones which are nouns. Can you help him?

table
bird
soft
jug
house
sing

Words can be put into groups according to the sort of work they do. Nouns are one of these groups.

A **noun** is a word that tells you the name of something.

If you can put "a", "an" or "the" in front of a word, that word is usually a noun.

"A", "an" and "the" have a group name too. They are called **articles.**

On the last day of school all the children in Mog and Zog's class come dressed as nouns. Write a list of these nouns on Miss Spell's noterock. Most of them are common nouns but there is one proper noun as well.

Don't forget to use capital letters for the proper noun.

The nouns in Zog's list are called common nouns. There is another group of nouns called proper nouns, which need to start with capital letters.

Miss Spell has given everyone a noun wordrock. They have to show which ones are proper nouns by crossing out the first letter and writing a capital letter in front of it. See if you can help Mog to complete her wordrock.

ogtown
cup
january
dog
mog
monday

The names of people and places are proper nouns.

The names of months and days are proper nouns too.

You can't usually put "the", "a" or "an" in front of a proper noun.

Miss Spell's Noterock

7

Pronouns

The Ogs and the Igs are on a trip to Ugton Towers amusement park. They are having a great time.

Come and see the strongman. Watch him lift two dinosaurs.

Instead of writing "Watch the strongman lift two dinosaurs" the signwriter has used "him" because it is already clear who the sentence is about.

The noun, the strongman, has been replaced by the pronoun "him".

Words that replace nouns are called **pronouns.**

All of these words are pronouns. You could use this list to help you complete the puzzle on the opposite page.

I	your	it
they	she	he
me	theirs	them
our	mine	you
its	yours	their
we	him	us
her	ours	his
my	hers	

When they got home, Zog wrote about their trip for the school magazine. The magazine's editor decided that his article was a little bit too long.

Zog realized that he could make it shorter by replacing some of the nouns with pronouns. He has underlined all the nouns that he wants to replace with pronouns. Can you write the correct pronouns above the nouns for him?

My family and the Ig family went to Ugton Towers. My family and the Igs had a wonderful time.

Grandpa liked the Wild Water. The Wild Water was Grandpa Og's best ride. Mig Ig preferred the Bucking Bronto. That was Mig Ig's best.

At lunch time Mr. Ig put a trick spider in Mrs. Ig's sandwich. Mrs. Ig was scared. Tig Ig laughed. Tig Ig thought it was very funny.

After lunch Ma and Pa went on the animal ride. A man collected Ma and Pa's tickets and then Ma and Pa were off.

Adjectives

The house next door to the Ogs has just been broken into. Luckily, Grandma Og was at home. She saw the robbers running away. This is what they looked like.

Grandma Og called Sergeant Stig of the Ogtown police. He came immediately. He wants to find out what the robbers looked like.

Sergeant Stig has asked Grandma to put a ring around the words on the rocks below, that best describe each robber. Can you help her?

Adjectives are words that describe nouns.

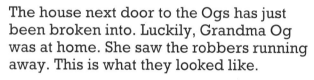

Robber 1

Height	tall	short
Hair	blonde	dark
	straight	curly
	long	short
Eyes	blue	brown
Nose	long	short
Ears	large	small
Clothes	scruffy	neat

Robber 2

Height	tall	short
Hair	blonde	dark
	straight	curly
	long	short
Eyes	blue	brown
Nose	long	short
Ears	large	small
Clothes	scruffy	neat

All the words that you have circled are adjectives.

Mr. Ug, who lives next door, is very upset when he discovers that he has been robbed. He draws a picture of everything that has been stolen to give to Sergeant Stig.

Sergeant Stig makes a list of the stolen items in his notebook. Can you fill in the adjectives he used to describe each item? He has made a note of the adjectives he wants to use on the opposite page.

Stolen goods

A _____ coin
A _____ vase
A _____ clock
A _____ hat
A _____ cup
A _____ necklace
A _____ picture

wooden
shoe
green
narrow
teapot
gold
square
straw
cheese
chipped

An adjective tells you more about a noun.

An adjective answers the question, "What is it like?"

An adjective usually comes before a noun.

There are three words on Sergeant Stig's list that are not adjectives. Which ones are they? Draw a ring around them.

Comparing

The Ogs enjoy gardening. They each have their own piece of garden where they grow vegetables as well as flowers. They are comparing the size of some of the vegetables they have grown. Can you fill in the missing words?

This bean is long.

This bean is longer.

This bean is the longest.

This carrot is short.

This carrot is _____

This carrot is the _____

The words at the end of these sentences are all **adjectives** - they tell you something about the nouns in the sentences.

Zog decides to try the carrots to see which one tastes the best. You can tell by his smile which one he likes the best.

Sometimes it sounds too awkward if you add "er" and "est" when you are comparing things. It sounds better to say "more beautiful" and "the most beautiful" rather than "beautifuler" and "beautifulest".

Longer words often sound awkward if you add "er" and "est".

This carrot is delicious.

This carrot is _____

This carrot is _____

12

Grandpa, Mrs. Og and Mog decide to have a competition to see who could grow the biggest and most beautiful sunflower. Mr. Og and Zog are the judges. Can you complete the judges' report by filling in the missing words?

Flower 1

Flower 2

Flower 3

Grandpa's flower

Mog's flower

Mrs. Og's flower

Judge's Report

Flower 1 is tall, but flower 2 is _____ and flower 3 is the _____.

The leaves on flower 2 are long, but those on flower 1 are _____ and those on flower 3 are the _____

There are many petals on flower 1, but there are _____ on flower 3. Flower 2 has the _____ petals.

Flower 1 is beautiful, but we feel that flower 2 is _____ _____ and flower 3 is the _____

We have therefore decided that although flower 1 is very good flower 2 is _____ and flower 3 is the _____

Be careful! A few words have a special pattern of their own, such as "bad", "worse", "the worst" and "many", "more", "the most".

GALWAY COUNTY

Adverbs

It is Zog's birthday and the Og family are playing an acting game. Each person has to pick a blue brick and a green brick and act the way the words tell them to.

Each of the blue bricks has a verb written on it. Each of the green bricks has a word that, when put with a verb, tells you more about the way that verb is done.

The Ogs are all acting out the words on the bricks. Can you guess who got which bricks? Write your answers on the chart below.

angrily

loudly

crawl

sleepily

Verbs tell you what a person or thing is being or doing.

Words that tell you more about the way a verb is done are called **adverbs.**

There should still be two empty spaces left next to one person. There are also two blank bricks. Look at that person and decide what you think should be written on the bricks. Fill in the bricks and finish the chart.

	blue	green
Mr. Og		
Mrs. Og		
Grandma		
Grandpa		
Mog		
Zog		

Verb Tenses

The Ogs are going to put on a show for their friends. Mog and Zog are watching Grandpa rehearse his juggling act. He has to rehearse every day.

I am juggling with fruit

Yesterday he juggled with rocks.

Tomorrow he will juggle with plates.

The words that have been underlined are all verbs, or parts of verbs.

Don't forget! Verbs are "doing" words.

The way you write a verb depends on whether you are writing about something that is happening now, something that has already happened, or something that is going to happen.

What has happened is called the past tense.

What is happening is called the present tense.

What will happen is called the future tense.

Look at the list below, then look at the pictures. Can you finish the sentences in the speech bubbles by writing the correct present tense phrase in each one? The first one has been done for you.

I am playing the stonepipe.

_____ with fruit.

dancing
playing
juggling
riding
spinning
walking

_____ plates on sticks.

_____ in a frilly dress.

You will need to use the future tense for the puzzle below.

_____ on stilts.

_____ a unicycle.

Use the information in the speech bubbles to finish writing this poster for the Ogs.

To make the future tense you usually write "will" before the verb.

Come to our show

Mr. Og _____

Zog Og _____

Grandma Og _____

_____

Mrs. Og _____

Mog Og _____

Grandpa Og _____

17

The past tense

Mog runs her own newspaper, called the Ogtown News. She is busy preparing things to go in the next issue. She is going to include pictures of some of the performers in the school concert. Underneath each picture she has written a sentence. Can you put the verb in each sentence into the past tense? Mog has already done one for you.

Mig Ig play$ed the stoneharp.

Tig Ig juggles with old shoes.

Sally Stig dances a jig.

Zog Og jumps through hoops.

Lucy Ug walks the tightrope.

Mog Og recites poems.

To change a present tense verb into a past tense verb you usually have to add "ed" or "d".

Not all verbs work like this. Mog has made up a crossword using words that don't. Can you think of the past tenses of all the words in the clues and fill in the answers in the crossword?

Across
1 fall
3 tell
5 buy
6 shake
7 throw
9 begin

Down
1 fight
2 lend
3 teach
4 grow
5 break
8 run

Verbs like these are called irregular verbs.

18

Zog has written an article about the robbery that took place in the house next door. He has written the article in the present tense, but Mog thinks it would be better to write it in the past tense. She has put yesterday at the beginning and underlined all the verbs she will need to change. She has changed the first one. Can you help her by doing the rest?

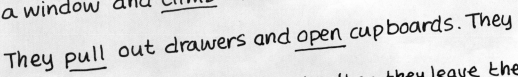

Ogtown News

Yesterday
~~Two robbers break~~ broke into

Mr. Ug's house. They <u>steal</u>

a number of valuable items.

The thieves <u>push</u> open

a window and <u>climb</u> in.

They <u>pull</u> out drawers and <u>open</u> cupboards. They

<u>hide</u> the stolen objects in sacks, then they <u>leave</u> the

house.

They <u>think</u> that no one <u>sees</u> them. They <u>are</u> wrong.

Grandma Og <u>looks</u> out of the window. She <u>gives</u>

Sergeant Stig a description of the two men. Later

that day Sergeant Stig <u>spots</u> the burglars. He <u>chases</u>

them and <u>catches</u> them.

Prepositions

Mog and Zog have organized a treasure hunt in the park for their friends. They have hidden ten chocolate coins wrapped in gold paper.

They have written some clues for their friends to use if they get stuck. The clues tell them where to look for the coins.

Can you finish off the clues by filling in the missing words?

Use the words from this list to help you.

You only need to use each word, or group of words, once.

among
inside
between
on top of
against
near
behind
under

the litter bins

the flowers

the tunnel

20

the merry-go-round · the goal post

the climbing net | the fence | the slide

21

J71834/428

Conjunctions

You will need to use one of these joining words:
and, or, but, because

The Ogtown Fire Fighters have been called to a fire in Dinosaur Drive. Everyone is very busy dealing with the emergency.

They are all speaking quickly and using short sentences. If there wasn't such a panic, they would probably be speaking in much longer sentences.

Can you make each person say one long sentence, instead of two short ones? Do this by putting a joining word between the two sentences. Write the long sentences in the empty speech bubble beside each person.

The Chief Fire Fighter's sentence has been written in already. The joining word in it is "because".

Is he all right? Should I fetch a doctor?

Let me through. I'm a nurse.

Run to the lake. Get some water.

Negatives

Milk is a fruit drink.

False. Milk is not a fruit drink.

An elephant is an insect.

Daffodils are yellow.

Bananas are vegetables.

Grandpa Og has made up a quiz for Zog and Mog and their friends. He reads a sentence to each person and they have to decide whether it is true or false. If it is true, they say "True" and repeat the sentence. If it is false they say "False" and say the sentence correctly.

Zog has had his turn. Can you fill in the rest of the answers?

If the sentence is false, you correct it by adding the word "not".

The parts of speech

Words such as "noun" and "adjective" are called the parts of speech. Mog has written down on her noterocks a list of parts of speech and their meanings to help her do her homework. Unfortunately, she trips over a stone and the noterocks break.

Can you help her piece together the rocks by drawing a line between each part of speech and its meaning?

If you can't remember what a word means, look back through the book until you find it.

nouns

adverbs

are little words like 'a', 'an' and 'the'

prepositions

are joining words

verbs

tell you more about a verb

articles

take the place of nouns

pronouns

are naming words

conjunctions

describe 'where' something is

adjectives

tell you more about a noun or pronoun

are doing words

This is Mog's homework. In the box under each word in the sentence below, she has to write down what part of speech that word is. Can you help her?

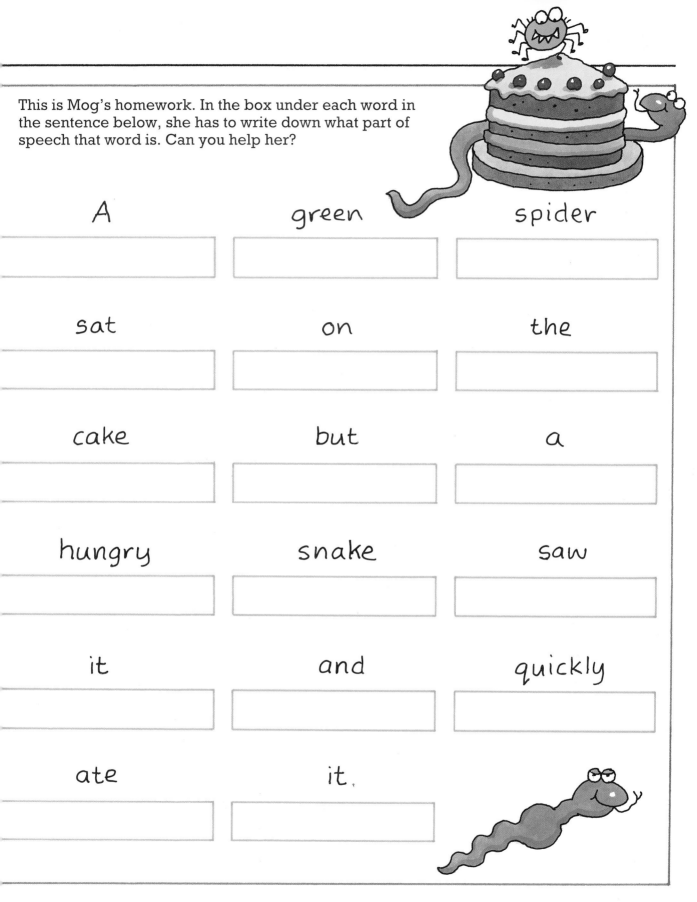

A

green

spider

sat

on

the

cake

but

a

hungry

snake

saw

it

and

quickly

ate

it.

Answers

Introducing grammar

Grammar is all about the way we use words. It involves choosing and arranging words so that they make sense for everybody. Words are usually used in groups called sentences. Each word in a sentence has a particular job to do. The puzzles in this book will help you to understand the job each word is doing.

Sentences

A sentence is a group of words that make complete sense on their own.

I went to a party

This is a sentence.

I went to a

This is not a sentence because it does not make sense.

Look at the groups of words below and put a star next to the ones that are sentences.

Never been there

I like swimming

She is clever ☆

He wrote a letter ☆

Please give him

Looked at me

Can you make up a sentence and write it in the space below?

Sentences can be very long, very short or somewhere in between.

This sentence is only two words.

Mog knits

This word tells you who the sentence is about. The person or thing that the sentence is about is called the **subject** of the sentence.

This word tells you what the person is doing. Words that tell you what someone or something is doing are called **verbs**.

Nearly all sentences have at least a subject and a verb.

The sentence above does not tell you very much. The sentence below gives you a bit more information.

Mog knits hats

This word tells you what is being knitted. The person or thing that the verb is happening to is called the **object** of the sentence.

Zog Og is trying to decide which of these words are verbs. Can you help him by putting a ring around the verbs?

street car (climb)

(laugh) horse

(throw) (dance)

(jump)

2

3

Can you use these words to make up a sentence about each of the Ogs?

writes a rockmobile a stonepipe Mrs. Og poems coins Mr. Og drives Zog Og mammoths eats Grandma Og Mog Og Grandpa Og plays swampburgers collects rides

Write your sentences here.

Grandpa Og (drives) a rockmobile

Grandma Og (plays) a stonepipe

Mr Og (eats) swampburgers

Mrs Og (collects) coins

Zog Og (rides) mammoths

Mog Og (writes) poems

Can you draw a straight line under the subject of each sentence?

Draw a ring around each verb.

Draw a wiggly line under the object in each sentence.

5

Nouns

Zog is daydreaming during a lesson at school. The teacher, Miss Spell, has written some words on the board. She asks Zog to put a star by the ones which are nouns. Can you help him?

table ☆
bird ☆
soft
jug ☆
house ☆
sing

Words can be put into groups according to the sort of work they do. Nouns are one of these groups.

A **noun** is a word that tells you the name of something.

If you can put "a", "an" or "the" in front of a word, that word is usually a noun.

"A", "an" and "the" are called **articles**.

On the last day of school all the children in Mog and Zog's class come dressed as nouns. Write a list of these nouns on Miss Spell's noterock. Most of them are common nouns but there is one proper noun as well.

Don't forget to use capital letters for the proper noun.

The nouns in Zog's list are called common nouns. There is another group of nouns called proper nouns, which need to start with capital letters.

Miss Spell has given everyone a noun wordrock. They have to show which ones are proper nouns by crossing out the first letter and writing a capital letter in front of it. See if you can help Mog to complete her wordrock.

Oogtown
cup
Jjanuary
dog
Mmog
Mmonday

The names of people and places are proper nouns.

The names of months and days are proper nouns too.

You can't usually put "the", "a" or "an" in front of a proper noun.

Miss Spell's	Noterock
flower	robot
apple	lion
witch	Santa Claus

6

7

Page 9

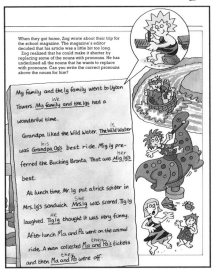

When they got home, Zog wrote about their trip for the school magazine. The magazine's editor decided that his article was a little bit too long. Zog realized that he could make it shorter by replacing some of the nouns with pronouns. He has underlined all the nouns that he wants to replace with pronouns. Can you write the correct pronouns above the nouns for him?

> My family and the Ig family went to Ugton
>   We
> Towers. <u>My family and the Igs</u> had a
> wonderful time.
> Grandpa liked the Wild Water. <u>The Wild Water</u>
>   his   it
> was <u>Grandpa Og's</u> best ride. Mig Ig pre-
>   her
> ferred the Bucking Bronto. That was <u>Mig Ig's</u>
> best.
> At lunch time Mr. Ig put a trick spider in
>   She
> Mrs. Ig's sandwich. <u>Mrs Ig</u> was scared. Tig Ig
> laughed. <u>Tig Ig</u> thought it was very funny.
> After lunch Ma and Pa went on the animal
>   their
> ride. A man collected <u>Ma and Pa's</u> tickets
>   they
> and then <u>Ma and Pa</u> were off.

Pages 10 and 11

Adjectives

The house next door to the Ogs has just been broken into. Luckily, Grandma Og was at home. She saw the robbers running away. This is what they looked like.

Grandma Og called Sergeant Stig of the Ogtown police. He came immediately. He wants to find out what the robbers looked like.

Sergeant Stig has asked Grandma to put a ring around the words on the rocks below, that best describe each robber. Can you help her?

Adjectives are words that describe nouns.

Robber 1
Height   (tall) short
Hair   blonde (dark)
     straight (curly)
Eyes   (long) short
     (blue) brown
Nose   long (short)
Ears   large (small)
Clothes   (scruffy) neat

Robber 2
Height   tall (short)
Hair   (blonde) dark
     straight (curly)
     long (short)
Eyes   blue (brown)
Nose   (long) short
Ears   (large) small
Clothes   scruffy (neat)

All the words that you have circled are adjectives.

Mr. Ug, who lives next door, is very upset when he discovers that he has been robbed. He draws a picture of everything that has been stolen to give to Sergeant Stig.

Sergeant Stig makes a list of the stolen items in his notebook. Can you fill in the adjectives he used to describe each item. He has made a note of the adjectives he wants to use on the opposite page.

Stolen goods
A <u>gold</u> coin   wooden
A <u>narrow</u> vase   (shoe)
A <u>wooden</u> clock   green
A <u>straw</u> hat   narrow
A <u>chipped</u> cup   gold (teapot)
A <u>green</u> necklace   straw (cheese)
A <u>square</u> picture   chipped

An adjective tells you more about a noun.

An adjective answers the question, "What is it like?"

An adjective usually comes before a noun.

There are three words on Sergeant Stig's list that are not adjectives. Which ones are they? Draw a ring around them.

Pages 12 and 13

Comparing

The Ogs enjoy gardening. They each have their own piece of garden where they grow vegetables as well as flowers. They are comparing the size of some of the vegetables they have grown. Can you fill in the missing words?

"This bean is long."
"This bean is longer."
"This bean is the longest."

"This carrot is short."
"This carrot is **shorter**"
"This carrot is **the shortest**"

The words at the end of these sentences are all **adjectives** - they tell you something about the nouns in the sentences.

Zog decides to try the carrots to see which one tastes the best. You can tell by his smile which one he likes the best.

Sometimes it sounds too awkward if you add "er" and "est" when you are comparing things. It sounds better to say "more beautiful" and "the most beautiful" rather than "beautifuler" and "beautifulest".

Longer words often sound awkward if you add "er" and "est".

"This carrot is delicious."
"This carrot is **more delicious**"
"This carrot is **most delicious**"

Grandpa, Mrs. Og and Mog decide to have a competition to see who could grow the biggest and most beautiful sunflower. Mr. Og and Zog are the judges. Can you complete the judges' report by filling in the missing words?

Flower 1   Flower 2   Flower 3

Grandpa's flower   Mog's flower   Mrs. Og's flower

Judge's Report
Flower 1 is tall, but flower 2 is <u>taller</u> and flower 3 is the <u>tallest</u>.

The leaves on flower 2 are long, but those on flower 1 are <u>longer</u> and those on flower 3 are the <u>longest</u>.

There are many petals on flower 1, but there are <u>more</u> on flower 3. Flower 2 has the <u>most</u> petals.

Flower 1 is beautiful, but we feel that flower 2 is <u>more beautiful</u> and flower 3 is the <u>most beautiful</u>.

We have therefore decided that although flower 1 is very good flower 2 is <u>better</u> and flower 3 is the <u>best</u>.

Be careful! A few words have a special pattern of their own, such as "bad", "worse", "the worst" and "many", "more", "the most".

12

13

Answers

Pages 14 and 15

Adverbs

It is Zog's birthday and the Og family are playing an acting game. Each person has to pick a blue brick and a green brick and act the way the words tell them to.

Each of the blue bricks has a verb written on it. Each of the green bricks has a word that, when put with a verb, tells you more about the way that verb is done.

The Ogs are all acting out the words on the bricks. Can you guess who got which bricks? Write your answers on the chart below.

Verbs tell you what a person or thing is being or doing.

Words that tell you more about the way a verb is done are called adverbs.

	blue	green
Mr. Og	sing	loudly
Mrs. Og	read	sadly
Grandma	crawl	quietly
Grandpa	sit	sleepily
Mog	write	happily
Zog	hop	angrily

There should still be two empty spaces left next to one person. There are also two blank bricks. Look at that person and decide what you think should be written on the bricks. Fill in the bricks and finish the chart.

Tree bricks: angrily, happily, sit, quietly, loudly, sing, read, write, hop, sadly, crawl, sleepily

Page 17

Look at the list below, then look at the pictures. Can you finish the sentences in the speech bubbles by writing the correct present tense phrase in each one? The first one has been done for you

dancing
playing
juggling
riding
spinning
walking

I am playing the stonepipe

I am juggling with fruit.

I am spinning plates on sticks.

I am dancing in a frilly dress.

You will need to use the future tense.

I am walking on stilts.

I am riding a unicycle.

To make the future tense you usually write "will" before the verb.

Use the information in the speech bubbles to finish writing this poster for the Ogs.

Come to our show

Mr. Og will spin plates on sticks.

Zog Og will walk on stilts.

Grandma Og will play the stonepipe

Mrs. Og will ride a unicycle

Mog Og will dance in a frilly dress

Grandpa Og will juggle with fruit.

Pages 18 and 19

The past tense

Mog runs her own newspaper, called the Ogtown News. She is busy preparing things to go in the next issue. She is going to include pictures of some of the performers in the school concert. Underneath each picture she has written a sentence. Can you put the verb in each sentence into the past tense? Mog has already done one for you.

Mig Ig played the stonepipe.

Tig Ig juggled with old shoes.

Sally Stig danced a jig.

Zog Og jumped through hoops.

Lucy Ug walked the tightrope.

Mog Og recited poems.

To change a present tense verb into a past tense verb you usually have to add "ed" or "d".

Not all verbs work like this. Mog has made up a crossword using words that don't. Can you think of the past tenses of all the words in the clues and fill in the answers in the crossword?

Verbs like these are called irregular verbs.

Across
1 fall
3 tell
5 buy
6 shake
7 throw
9 begin

Down
1 fight
2 lend
3 teach
4 grow
5 break
8 run

Crossword answers:
fell, told, bought, shook, threw, began

Zog has written an article about the robbery that took place in the house next door. He has written the article in the present tense, but Mog thinks it would be better to write it in the past tense. She has put yesterday at the beginning and underlined all the verbs she will need to change. She has changed the first one. Can you help her by doing the rest?

Ogtown News

Yesterday ~~Two robbers break into~~ broke into Mr. Ug's house. They ~~steal~~ stole a number of valuable items. The thieves ~~push~~ pushed open a window and ~~climb in~~ climbed in. They ~~pull~~ pulled out drawers and ~~open~~ opened cupboards. They ~~hide~~ hid the stolen objects in sacks, then they ~~leave~~ left the house.

They ~~think~~ thought that no one ~~sees~~ saw them. They ~~are~~ were wrong. Grandma Og ~~looks~~ looked out of the window. She ~~gives~~ gave Sergeant Stig a description of the two men. Later that day Sergeant Stig ~~spots~~ spotted the burglars. He ~~chases~~ chased them and ~~catches~~ caught them.

30

Answers

Pages 24 and 25

Negatives

Milk is a fruit drink.

False. Milk is not a fruit drink.

True. Sea water is salty.

False. An elephant is not an insect.

An elephant is an insect.

Sea water is salty.

False. Fish do not live in space.

True. A hat is worn on your head.

True. Daffodils are yellow.

Daffodils are yellow.

Fish live in space.

A hat is worn on your head.

False. Baby cats are not called catlets.

Bananas are vegetables.

Baby cats are called catlets.

False. Bananas are not vegetables.

Grandpa Og has made up a quiz for Zog and Mog and their friends. He reads a sentence to each person and they have to decide whether it is true or false. If it is true, they say "True" and repeat the sentence. If it is false they say "False" and say the sentence correctly.

Zog has had his turn. Can you fill in the rest of the answers?

If the sentence is false, you correct it by adding the word "not".

Words like "no" and "not" are called **negatives.**

24   25

Pages 26 and 27

The parts of speech

Words such as "noun" and "adjective", are called the parts of speech. Mog has written down on her noterocks a list of parts of speech and their meanings to help her do her homework. Unfortunately, she trips over a stone and the noterocks break.

Can you help her piece together the rocks by drawing a line between each part of speech and its meaning?

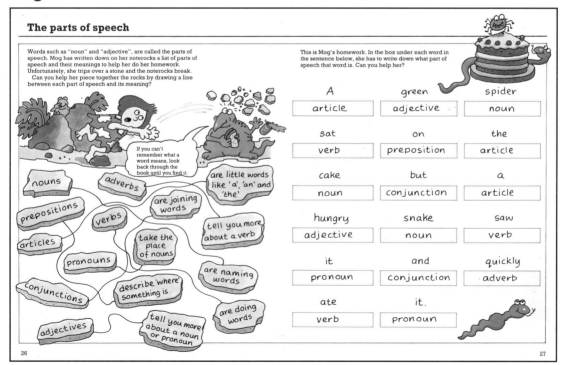

If you can't remember what a word means, look back through the book until you find it.

nouns

adverbs

are little words like 'a', 'an' and 'the'

prepositions

are joining words

verbs

tell you more about a verb

take the place of nouns

articles

pronouns

are naming words

conjunctions

describe 'where' something is

are doing words

adjectives

tell you more about a noun or pronoun

This is Mog's homework. In the box under each word in the sentence below, she has to write down what part of speech that word is. Can you help her?

A	green	spider
article	adjective	noun

sat	on	the
verb	preposition	article

cake	but	a
noun	conjunction	article

hungry	snake	saw
adjective	noun	verb

it	and	quickly
pronoun	conjunction	adverb

ate	it.	
verb	pronoun	

26   27